GW01144864

This edition published in 2015 by Pikku Publishing
54 Ferry Street
London E14 3DT
www.pikkupublishing.com

ISBN: 978-0-9928050-5-0

Copyright in this edition © 2015 Pikku Publishing

First published by the University of London Press Ltd in 1936

Pikku Publishing and Dr Frances Grundy, heir to the estate of Elizabeth Clark, wish to state that they have used all reasonable endeavours to establish copyright. If you would like to contact the Publisher, please write to Pikku Publishing.

1 3 5 7 9 10 8 6 4 2

Printed in China by Toppan Leefung Printing Ltd

All rights reserved. No part of this publication may be reproduced, stored in a retrieval system, or transmitted in any form or by any means, electronic, mechanical, photocopying, recording or otherwise, without the prior permission of the publishers and copyright holders.

While every care has been taken to ensure the information contained in this book is as accurate as possible, the authors and publishers can accept no responsibility for any loss, injury or inconvenience sustained by any person using the advice contained herein.

AUTHOR'S NOTE

The tales in this little book and its companions are reprinted from various collections of stories for storytellers which I have written during the past ten years.

It has been very often suggested to me that children would enjoy reading these stories quite as much as (I am happy to believe) they have hitherto enjoyed hearing them read or told. Accordingly, some of the stories have been chosen.

I hope that these small books may bring pleasure to innumerable small people, at home, at school, or wherever they and the books may be.

ELIZABETH CLARK

CONTENTS

	PAGE
THE TALE OF A TURNIP	7
THE TALE OF THE HARVEST BUN	13
THE LITTLE BROWN BIRD	25
THE OLD WOMAN WHO LIVED IN A VINEGAR BOTTLE	33
FATHER SPARROW'S TUG-OF-WAR	45
THE CAT THAT CLIMBED THE CHRISTMAS TREE	54
QUESTIONS	62

THE TALE OF A TURNIP

Chapter One: Turnip Seed

ONCE upon a time there was a little old House, and in it lived a little old Man.

A little old Woman lived there too. She was his wife.

The little old Man and the little old Woman had a little Girl living with them. She was their grandchild.

The little Girl had a little black-and-white Cat, and there was a little Mouse too; but nobody knew where her hole was, except the little black-and-white Cat.

They all lived together in the little old House.

One day the little old Man said to the little old Woman:

" I am going out to the field to plant a seed."
" What kind of a seed ? "
" A turnip seed."

So the little old Man went out to the field, and dug a little hole. He put in a seed. Then he went back to the House and said to the little old Woman:

" I have planted it ! "

They both said, " We hope it will grow."

It did grow. The sun shone, and the wind blew, and the rain rained. A little green shoot came out of the ground, and it grew and grew and grew and *grew*, till it grew to a very big turnip.

One day the little old Man said to the little old Woman:

" Put the pot on the fire and boil some water. Mind it is a big pot, for I am going to pull up the turnip, and we will all have turnip soup."

Chapter Two : Turnip Up

THE little old Woman made up the fire, and took the biggest pot she had, and filled it with water, and put it on the fire to boil the water to make the turnip soup.

While she was doing this, the little old Man went out to the field and caught hold of the turnip. He pulled and pulled and pulled and *pulled*. But he could not pull up the turnip.

So the little old Man called to the little old Woman :

" Come and take hold of me, so that we may pull up the turnip."

The little old Woman left the pot boiling on the fire, and came running out of the house. She took hold of the little old Man. The little old Man took hold of the turnip, and they pulled and pulled and pulled and pulled and *pulled*. But they could not pull up the turnip.

So the little old Woman called to the little Girl :

" Come and take hold of me, so that we may pull up the turnip."

The little Girl came running out of the house. She took hold of the little old Woman. The little old Woman took hold of the little old

Man. The little old Man took hold of the turnip, and they pulled and pulled and pulled and *pulled*. But they could not pull up the turnip.

So the little Girl, the grandchild, called to the little black-and-white Cat:

" Come and take hold of me so that we may pull up the turnip."

The little black-and-white Cat came running out of the house with its tail in the air, as little cats do when they are pleased. She took hold of the little Girl. The little Girl took hold of the little old Woman. The little old Woman took hold of the little old Man. The little old Man took hold of the turnip, and they pulled and pulled and pulled and *pulled*. But they could *not* pull up the turnip.

So the little black-and-white Cat called to the little Mouse :

" Come and take hold of me so that we may pull up the turnip."

Chapter Three : Turnip Soup

THE little Mouse popped out of her hole. She took hold of the little black-and-white Cat.

The little black-and-white Cat took hold of the little Girl. The little Girl took hold of the little old Woman. The little old Woman took hold of the little old Man. The little old Man took hold of the turnip, and they pulled and pulled and pulled and *pulled*—and up came the turnip.

The little old Man fell over on top of the little old Woman. The little old Woman, his wife, fell over on top of the little Girl. The little Girl fell over on top of the little black-and-white Cat. The little black-and-white Cat fell over on top of the little Mouse—and on top of them all was the turnip. But nobody was hurt.

It was a very good turnip, and it made very good turnip soup. There was enough for the little old Man, and the little old Woman, and the little Girl, and the little black-and-white Cat, and the little Mouse too. They all had enough, and there was still enough left over for one.

They could not make up their minds who should have that.

The little old Woman said the little old Man ought to have it, because it was his turnip.

The little old Man said the little old Woman ought to have it, because it was her soup.

They both said the little Girl ought to have it, because she was growing so fast.

The little Girl said the little black-and-white Cat ought to have it, because she had such nice whiskers.

The little black-and-white Cat said the little Mouse ought to have it, because it was she who pulled it up.

Which do you vote for?

The Tale of the Harvest Bun

Chapter One: The Bun that Sang

ONCE upon a time a mother was baking harvest buns. A harvest bun is something like bread, but it has currants in it, and sugar, and candied peel, and spice. When it comes out of the oven it looks like a big brown bun, and it smells good and tastes better.

Well, the mother was baking harvest buns. Next day the corn was to be cut. Everybody would be busy and everybody would be hungry, so the oven was full and smelled as sweet as could be. The father sniffed, and the boy and girl sniffed, and they all thought, " How good they will taste to-morrow ! "

Presently the mother opened the oven door and peeped in.

" The bun on the top shelf is beginning to burn," she said. " I had better take it out."

She pulled out the baking tin and it burnt her hand. She gave a little squeak and nearly dropped the tin. Out bounced the harvest bun, and down to the floor it fell. And would you believe it : instead of lying there flat upon the floor it gave a hop and a skip and a jump and began to roll towards the door.

Out of the door it went, and as it went it sang to itself. This is what it sang :

" I'm a harvest bun,
  I'm a curranty bun,
  And I roll and run,
  I roll and I run.
  The father and mother,
  The sister and brother,
  They ALL run after the harvest bun."

At first they were all too surprised to move.

Then they ran as fast as they could, but they *couldn't* catch up with the harvest bun.

Chapter Two : Out and Away

As the bun rolled through the farmyard it met a duck. The duck looked at the bun with her little black eye, and thought how nice it would be to eat.

"Quack! quack!" she said. "Where are you going?"

But the bun never stopped. It did not want to be eaten by a duck, so it rolled on faster and faster, and sang to itself again. This is what it sang:

"I'm a harvest bun,
　I'm a curranty bun,
　And I roll and run,
　I roll and I run.
　The father and mother,
　The sister and brother,
　The duck makes another,
　They ALL run after the harvest bun."

Away they all went, and the duck waddled after, but they *couldn't* catch up with the harvest bun.

As the bun rolled out of the farmyard gate it met a hen. The hen looked at the bun with her head on one side and she thought it looked very nice to eat.

" Cluck ! cluck ! " she said. " Where are you going ? "

But the bun never stopped. It did not want to be eaten by a hen, so it rolled on faster and faster, and sang to itself again. This is what it sang :

" I'm a harvest bun,
I'm a curranty bun,
And I roll and run,
I roll and I run.
The father and mother,
The sister and brother,
The duck makes another,
The hen flaps above her,
They ALL run after the harvest bun."

Away they went again. First came the people running, then the duck quacking. Last

"HULLO! HULLO!" HE SAID, "WHERE ARE YOU GOING?"

came the hen flapping and cackling along behind. But they *couldn't* catch up with the harvest bun.

The bun rolled out of the farmyard into a lane, and there it met Old-Man-John hobbling along. Old-Man-John looked at it and he thought it looked very nice and brown.

" Hullo ! hullo ! " he said. " Where are you going ? "

But the bun never stopped. It did not want to be eaten by Old-Man-John, so it rolled on faster and faster, and sang to itself again. This is what it sang :

" I'm a harvest bun,
I'm a curranty bun,
And I roll and run,
I roll and I run.
The father and mother,
The sister and brother,
The duck makes another,
The hen flaps above her,
And Old-Man-John
Comes hurrying on,
They ALL run after the harvest bun."

Away they went. First came the people running, then the duck quacking, then the hen flapping, and then Old-Man-John hobbling along behind, and the duck was last of all. But they *couldn't* catch up with the harvest bun.

Chapter Three : Out in the Lane

THE bun went rolling down the lane and there it met a horse. The horse thought it smelled very nice.

" Clip-clop ! " he said. " Where are you going ? "

But the bun never stopped. It did not want to be eaten by a horse, so it rolled on faster and faster, and sang to itself again. This is what it sang :

" I'm a harvest bun,
 I'm a curranty bun,
 And I roll and run,
 I roll and I run.
 The father and mother,
 The sister and brother,
 The duck makes another,

The hen flaps above her,
And Old-Man-John
Comes hurrying on,
And the horse trots along,
They ALL run after the harvest bun."

Away they went. The horse trotted in front, then came the people running, then the duck quacking, then the hen flapping, and then Old-Man-John hobbling along behind. But they *couldn't* catch up with the harvest bun.

As the bun rolled by a field of grass a cow looked over the hedge. She thought it a beautiful bun.

"Moo, moo!" she said. "Where are you going?"

But the bun never stopped. It did not want to be eaten by a cow, so it rolled on faster and faster, and sang to itself again. This is what it sang:

"I'm a harvest bun,
I'm a curranty bun,
And I roll and run,
I roll and I run.

The father and mother,
The sister and brother,
The duck makes another,
The hen flaps above her,
And Old-Man-John
Comes hurrying on,
And the horse trots along,
The cow says, ' Moo ! '
And she's coming too,
They ALL run after the harvest bun."

Away they went. First came the horse trotting, then the people running, then the duck quacking, then the hen flapping, then Old-Man-John hobbling, and then the cow mooing along behind. But they *couldn't* catch up with the harvest bun.

Chapter Four : Gobble Gobble

AT last the harvest bun came to the bottom of the lane, and it rolled round a corner, and there was the river. The harvest bun did not know what to do. Nobody could roll upon a river.

"I'm a Harvest Bun and I'm not very big   Please carry me over dear Mr Pig"

But just then, up trotted a fine fat pig. When the fine fat pig saw the harvest bun he thought it looked beautiful and plump and brown.

"Humph, humph!" he said. "What are you doing *here*?"

The harvest bun was really rather

tired of rolling. It said in a very quiet voice :

"I'm a harvest bun,
And I'm not very big.
Please carry me over,
Dear Mr. Pig."

"Of course I will," said the pig. "Jump on my back."

The harvest bun gave a hop and a skip and it jumped on to the pig's back.

"The water is very deep," said the pig. "I think you had better come up higher."

The harvest bun gave a hop and a skip and jumped on to the pig's head.

"The water is very wet," said the pig. "I think you had better come inside."

Then he tossed up his head, and caught the harvest bun in his mouth, and gobbled it up, and went splashing across the river.

I don't suppose the harvest bun minded at all, do you? Harvest buns are made to be eaten, and he was a nice fat comfortable pig.

The horse, the father and mother, the sister

and brother, the duck and the hen and Old-Man-John and the cow all came round the corner. They were just in time to see the fine fat pig gobble up the harvest bun. So they all turned round and went home again.

The horse and the cow went back to their fields, and the rest went back to the farm, and Old-Man-John went too. All the other harvest buns were baked and brown, and next day when the corn was cut everyone had harvest buns for lunch and tea.

THE LITTLE BROWN BIRD

Chapter One:
The Silver Birch

Once upon a time in the Land of Long Ago there was a Little Brown Bird, and he was very unhappy because he had broken his wing. That was bad enough. He did not like to have to go hop, hop, hop until his wing got well, instead of flying through the air.

Worse still, winter was coming. Soon the North Wind would go roaring through the woods, shaking the leaves from the trees, bringing the snow, and covering the blue sky with grey clouds. All the little brown bird's friends were saying, "Winter is coming. Winter is coming. We must go, go, go."

What would the poor Little Brown Bird do

without them? Each day some of them spread their wings and flew away to warm countries where the sun shone, and there were leaves on the trees and flowers in the grass, and plenty of food for little birds to eat all through the winter. Every day more and more went, till at last the Little Brown Bird was left all alone, and he was very unhappy indeed.

"What shall I do?" said the Little Brown Bird. "What shall I do with no friends to talk to all through the long cold winter?"

Then he had a bright idea. "I will go and ask a tree to take care of me till the spring comes back again," he said.

So off he went, hop, hop, hop, with his broken wing, till he came to the Silver Birch tree.

Now the Silver Birch is a very pretty tree with a silvery white trunk. It has long slender branches that wave in the wind, and little green leaves that twinkle when the sun shines on them. The Little Brown Bird said to himself, " What a pretty lady ! She is sure to be kind to me."

He called to her :

" Lady Birch ! Lady Birch ! I am a Little Brown Bird with a broken wing. All the other birds have gone away and left me. May I sit among your branches till the spring comes back again ? "

But the Silver Birch was not kind to him at all. She just looked at him and fluttered all her leaves and said, " Certainly not. Go away, Little Bird. I never talk to strange little birds."

Chapter Two : Grumbles and Tears

THE Little Brown Bird was very disappointed, but he said to himself :

" I must find a tree to sit in."

So he went away, hop, hop, hop, with his broken wing, till he came to the great big Oak tree.

Now the Oak is very big and strong, with

branches that spread out far and wide. When the Little Brown Bird looked at him he said to himself:

"He looks so big and strong, he *must* be kind."

He called to him:

"Father Oak! Father Oak! I'm a Little Brown Bird with a broken wing. All the other birds have gone away and left me. May I sit among your branches till the spring comes back again?"

But the Oak was feeling very cross that morning, for he had a pain in his roots. So he said in his big voice, "Certainly *not*. If I let you sit among my branches you might eat my acorns."

The Little Brown Bird was very disappointed, but he said to himself:

"I *must* find a tree to sit in."

So he went away, hop, hop, hop, with his broken wing, till he came to the Weeping Willow, who was bending and bowing and trailing her branches in the river.

The Little Brown Bird said to himself:

"She looks rather sad. Perhaps she will be kind to me."

He called to her:

" Lady Willow ! Lady Willow ! I am a Little Brown Bird with a broken wing. All the other birds have gone away and left me. May I sit among your branches till the spring comes back again ? "

But the Weeping Willow only waved her branches and spoke in a sad and weary tone:

" Go away, Little Bird. I have troubles of my own ! "

The poor Little Brown Bird was so unhappy that he really didn't know what to do. He sat there with all his brown feathers fluffed out, looking very miserable indeed. He really felt as if he must curl up into a little brown ball and cry.

And then he heard a voice.

Chapter Three : Little Bird's Friends

IT was a kind voice, and a warm voice, and it was speaking to him:

" Little Bird ! Little Bird ! My branches

are thick and cosy. Will you hop up and keep warm among them till the spring comes back again?"

The Little Brown Bird looked to see who was talking to him. It was the kind of Fir tree that is called a Spruce. Sometimes we make it into a Christmas-tree. It looked thick and warm, and he hopped up into its branches. They were so comfortable and cosy that he thought he would put his head under the wing that was not broken, and go fast asleep.

But just then he heard another voice. It was rather a creaky voice, but very kind, and it was speaking to him:

"Little Bird! Little Bird. I can keep the wind off."

Little Brown Bird peeped out to see who was talking. It was the tall Pine tree that we call

"GO AWAY, LITTLE BIRD, I'VE GOT TROUBLES OF MY OWN."

the Spruce tree's branches, and the Scots Pine took care of him, and he put his head under the wing that was not broken, and went fast asleep.

That night the North Wind went roaring through the woods. He blew Lady Silver Birch about till her pretty green leaves came down and lay in a golden shower round her silver trunk. He tossed Father Oak till the pain in his roots was worse than ever, and all his leaves and his acorns were lying on the ground. He sent all the Weeping Willow's leaves floating down the river.

But he never touched the Spruce Fir or the Scots Pine or the Juniper tree. They stayed fresh and green all the winter, to take care of the Little Brown Bird. And the Little Brown Bird's broken wing got well and strong, so that he could fly about with the other birds when spring came back again.

The OLD WOMAN WHO LIVED in a VINEGAR-BOTTLE

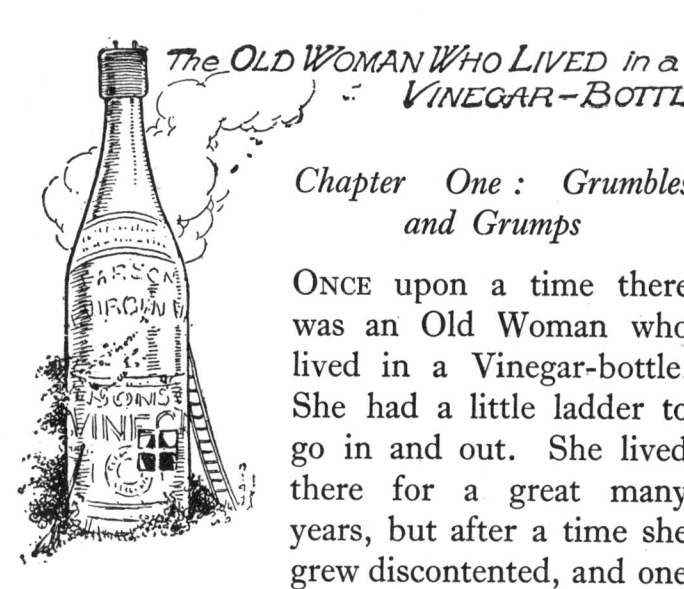

Chapter One : Grumbles and Grumps

ONCE upon a time there was an Old Woman who lived in a Vinegar-bottle. She had a little ladder to go in and out. She lived there for a great many years, but after a time she grew discontented, and one day she began to grumble. She grumbled so loud that a Fairy heard her as she was passing by.

"Oh dear! Oh dear! Oh dear!" said the Old Woman. "I ought not to live in a Vinegar-bottle. 'Tis a shame, so it is, 'tis a shame. I ought to live in a nice little white house, with pink curtains at the windows, and roses and honeysuckle growing over it, and there ought to be flowers and vegetables in the garden and a pig in a sty. Yes, there ought. 'Tis a shame, so it is. 'Tis a shame."

The Fairy was sorry for her because she lived in a Vinegar-bottle.

"Never you mind," she said. "When you go to bed to-night, just you turn round three times, and when you wake up in the morning you will see what you will see."

The Old Woman went to bed in the Vinegar-bottle and she turned round three times, though there was very little room to do it. And when she woke up in the morning, she was in a little white bed in a room with pink curtains.

She jumped out of bed, and ran across the room, and pulled aside the pink curtains and looked out of the window. Yes, it was! It was a little white house with roses and honeysuckle, and there was a garden with flowers and vegetables, and there was a pig. She could hear it grunting in the sty.

The Old Woman was pleased. But she forgot something she ought not to have forgotten.

Chapter Two : *The Little Red House*

WHAT was it the Old Woman forgot? She forgot to say "Thank you" to the Fairy.

The Fairy went East and she went West. She went North and she went South as well; and one day she came back to where the Old Woman was living in the little white house with pink curtains at the windows, and roses and honeysuckle and flowers and vegetables in the garden, and the pig in the sty.

"I will just go and take a look at her," the Fairy said to herself. "She *will* be pleased."

But as the Fairy passed by the Old Woman's window, she could hear the Old Woman talking to herself. What do you think she was saying?

"Oh! 'tis a shame," said the Old Woman, "'tis a shame. So it is, 'tis a shame. Why should I live in a poky little cottage? Other folk live in little red-brick houses on the edge of the town where they can watch who goes by to market. Why shouldn't I live in a little red-brick house on the edge of the town and see the folk going by to market? I am getting too old to do my own work, too. I ought to have a little maid to wait on me. So I did. Oh, 'tis a shame, 'tis a shame. 'Tis a *shame*."

The Fairy was sorry, because she had hoped the Old Woman would have been pleased.

But she said, "Well, never you mind. When you go to bed to-night, just you turn round three times, and when you wake up in the morning you will see what you will see."

So the Old Woman went to bed in the little white house with the pink curtains at the windows and the roses and honeysuckle, and the flowers and vegetables in the garden, and the pig in the sty. She turned round three times.

When she woke up in the morning, someone was standing by the bed.

"Please, mum, I have brought you a cup of tea."

The Old Woman opened her eyes and looked, and there was a little maid to help her do her work. She had brought the Old Woman a cup of tea to drink before she got out of bed.

When the Old Woman had drunk her tea, she got up and looked out of the window. Yes, it was! It was a little red-brick house, and it was on the edge of the town. She could see the folk going by to market.

The Old Woman was pleased. But once more she forgot to say "Thank you" to the Fairy.

The Fairy went East and she went West. She went North and she went South as well, and one day she came back to where the Old Woman was living in the little red-brick house, on the edge of the town, where she could see the folk going by to market. "I will just go and take a look at her," the Fairy said to herself. "She *will* be pleased!"

But when the Fairy stood on the Old Woman's door-step, she could hear the Old Woman talking to herself. (The Fairy was not listening at the key-hole, but it was just as high as her ear and she could not help hearing what came through.)

What do you think the Old Woman was saying?

"Oh! 'tis a shame," said the Old Woman, "'tis a shame, so it is. 'Tis a shame. Why should I live in a little house, when other folks live in big houses in the middle of the town, with white steps up to the door, and men and maids to wait on them, and a carriage and pair to go driving in ? Why shouldn't I live in a big house in the middle of the town, with white steps up to the door, and men and maids to wait on me, and a carriage and pair to go driving in ? 'Tis a shame, 'tis a shame, so it is. *'Tis* a shame ! "

The Fairy was disappointed, because she had hoped the Old Woman would have been pleased. But she said, " Well, never you mind. When you go to bed to-night, just you turn round three times, and when you wake up in the morning you will see what you will see."

Chapter Three : The Big House

THE Old Woman went to bed that night in the little red-brick house on the edge of the town, where she could see the folk going by to market. She turned round three times, and when she woke up in the morning she was in the grandest bed she had ever seen. It had brass knobs at the top and brass knobs at the bottom; the Old Woman had never seen a bed like that before.

When she got up and looked out of the window—yes, it was! It was a big house in the middle of the town, and there were white steps up to the door, and men and maids to wait on her, and a carriage and pair to go driving in.

The Old Woman was pleased. But still she forgot to say "Thank you" to the Fairy.

The Fairy went East and she went West. She went North and she went South as well; and one day she came back to the town where the Old Woman was living in the big house in the middle of the town, with white steps up to the door, and men and maids to wait on her, and a carriage and pair to go driving in.

"I will just go and take a look at her," the Fairy said to herself. "She *will* be pleased."

But as soon as the Fairy stood inside the Old Woman's door, she could hear the Old Woman talking to herself. What do you think she was saying?

"Oh! 'tis a shame," said the Old Woman,

" 'tis a shame, so it is. 'Tis a shame. Look at the Queen, sitting on a gold throne and living in a Palace, with a gold crown on her head, and red velvet carpet to walk on. Why shouldn't I be a Queen and sit on a gold throne and live in a Palace, with a gold crown on my head and red velvet carpet to walk on ? 'Tis a shame, 'tis a shame, so it is. 'Tis a *shame*."

The Fairy was disappointed, because she had hoped the Old Woman would have been pleased. But she said, " Well, never you mind. When you go to bed to-night, just you turn round three times, and when you wake up in the morning you will see what you will see."

The Old Woman went to sleep in the grand bed with the brass knobs at the top and the brass knobs at the bottom, in the big house in the middle of the town, with white steps up to the door, and men and maids to wait on her, and a carriage and pair to go driving in.

She turned round three times, and when she woke up in the morning she was very surprised indeed.

Chapter Four : The Biggest Surprise of All

No wonder the Old Woman was surprised. She was in the grandest bed that ever was seen. It had a red satin coverlet, and there was a red velvet carpet by the side of the bed, and a gold crown on a table all ready to put on when she dressed.

The Old Woman got up and dressed, and put on the gold crown, and walked on the red velvet carpet, and sat on a throne of gold.

The Old Woman was pleased. But even then she forgot to say " Thank you " to the Fairy.

The Fairy went East and she went West. She went North and she went South as well ; and one day she came back to the town where the Old Woman was living in the palace, with a gold crown on her head, and a gold throne to sit on, and a red velvet carpet to walk on.

" I will just go and take a look at her," the Fairy said to herself. " She *will* be pleased."

So she walked right in at the palace door, and up the red velvet stairs, till she came to the Old Woman sitting on a gold throne with a gold crown on her head. As soon as the Old Woman saw the Fairy she opened her mouth, and what do you think she said?

" Oh! 'tis a shame," said the Old Woman, " 'tis a shame, so it is. 'Tis a shame. This throne is most uncomfortable. The crown is too heavy for my head, and there is a draught down the back of my neck. This is a most uncomfortable palace. Why can't I get a home to suit me? 'Tis a shame, 'tis a shame, so it is. *'Tis* a shame."

" Oh, very well," said the Fairy. " If all you want is just a home to suit you, when you go to bed to-night, just you turn round three times, and when you wake up in the morning you will see what you will see."

The Old Woman went to bed that night in the palace, in the big bed with the red satin coverlet, and the red velvet carpet by the side of the bed, and the gold crown on a table all ready to put on in the morning. She turned round three times. There was plenty of room to do it.

When she woke up in the morning, where do you think she was? She was back in the Vinegar-bottle. And she stayed there the rest of her life.

" 'TIS A SHAME, THE CROWN IS TOO HEAVY FOR MY HEAD."

"I shall stay here just as long as I please," he said lazily.

Father Sparrow was telling Mother Sparrow all about it, when suddenly—*bump!* Somebody very big crashed against the tree. It rocked and swayed so that Father Sparrow nearly fell off his twig; and if Mother Sparrow had not sat very tight the eggs would have rolled out of the nest.

"Really there is no peace in the forest this morning," said Father Sparrow. "Now, who can that be?"

He flew down to see. What he saw was a big grey back and a little grey tail going away amongst the trees. It was Brother Elephant taking a walk in the forest.

"Stop, Brother Elephant!" chirped Father Sparrow. "Do you know that you nearly shook my wife off her nest?"

"Well," said Brother Elephant, "I don't mind if I did."

"You don't mind!" twittered Father Sparrow. "You don't mind! I'll make you mind, Brother Elephant. If you shake my nest again, I will tie you up!"

Mother Sparrow gave a little chirp. Brother Elephant chuckled.

"Tie me up then," he said. "You are quite welcome to do it; but you can't keep me tied, Father Sparrow, not even if a thousand sparrows tried."

"Wait and see," said Father Sparrow.

Brother Elephant trumpeted and went crashing through the forest. After a little talk with Mother Sparrow, Father Sparrow flew down to the river. The Crocodile was still there, fast asleep and filling up all the bathing-place. Father Sparrow chirped and the Crocodile opened one eye.

"I like this place," he said.

"You may like it," said Father Sparrow, "but I can tell you this, if I find you here to-morrow I will tie you up."

"You may tie me as much as you like," said the Crocodile, shutting his eye again, "but you can't keep me tied, Father Sparrow—not if a thousand sparrows tried."

"Wait and see," chirped Father Sparrow. "Wait and see."

Chapter Two : Father Sparrow's Plan

FATHER SPARROW was very busy all that morning, talking to all his sparrow friends. Next day they were all up very early and working hard. There were quite a thousand of them, and they had a long piece of creeper, nearly as strong as the strongest rope.

Presently Brother Elephant came crashing through the forest. *Bump!* he went against Father Sparrow's tree.

"Well," said Brother Elephant, "here I am. Are you going to tie me up, Father Sparrow?"

"Yes," chirped Father Sparrow. "I am going to tie you up *and* hold you tight."

Then he and all the other sparrows pulled, and pecked, and hopped, and tugged, and fluttered till the creeper rope was tight round Brother Elephant's big body.

"Now, Brother Elephant," said Father Sparrow, "when I say 'Pull,' *pull*."

"So I will," said Brother Elephant.

Father Sparrow and all the other sparrows flew away with the rope to the riverside. There was the Crocodile.

"Have you and your friends come to tie me up, Father Sparrow?" he said.

"Yes," said Father Sparrow. "I am going to tie you up *and* hold you tight."

"Tie away," said the Crocodile. Then the sparrows pulled, and pecked, and chattered, and tugged, and hopped, till the rope was tight round the Crocodile's long body.

"Now," said Father Sparrow, "when I say 'Pull,' *pull*."

Then Father Sparrow perched himself on the middle of the rope among the bushes. Neither Brother Elephant nor the Crocodile could see him, and they could not see one another. "*Pull!*" cried Father Sparrow in a very loud chirp.

Brother Elephant gave a great tug.

"That will surprise Father Sparrow," he said. But it was Brother Elephant who was surprised. From the other end of the line came a jerk that nearly pulled him off his feet.

The Crocodile was surprised, too, and no wonder; for they both thought it was Father Sparrow pulling.

"What a strong sparrow he is!" said the Crocodile.

"WHAT A STRONG SPARROW HE IS!" SAID THE CROCODILE.

"How hard Father Sparrow can pull!" said Brother Elephant, and they both pulled and pulled and pulled and *pulled*.

Sometimes Brother Elephant pulled hardest

and the Crocodile was nearly pulled out of the river. Sometimes the Crocodile gave a jerk, and Brother Elephant had to twist his trunk round a tree and hold on. Neither could move the other an inch. It was a wonderful tug-of-war.

The sun rose high in the sky and began to creep down towards the west. They grew hot and thirsty and tired. The sparrows laughed at them when they puffed and grunted and panted.

Each of them thought, " I wish I had not laughed at Father Sparrow."

But still they pulled and pulled and pulled and *pulled*.

At last, just as the sun was beginning to slip out of sight, Brother Elephant spoke in a very small voice :

" Please tell Father Sparrow that if he will stop pulling and untie me, I will never be rude to him again."

Just at the same moment the Crocodile said, " Please, Father Sparrow, stop pulling and untie me, and I will never take your bathing-place again."

"HE WAS SO ASHAMED OF BEING BEATEN BY FATHER SPARROW."

"Very well," chirped Father Sparrow very loudly. "Very well, very well!" (That was the same for him as "Hip, hip, hurrah!")

The sparrows hopped, and pecked, and pulled, and chattered till they untied Brother Elephant, and he went away with his head down. He was so ashamed of being beaten by Father Sparrow.

They untied the Crocodile too, and he crawled in among the high reeds by the river and hid himself. He was very cross because he had been tied up all day.

After that Brother Elephant walked quietly in the forest, and the Crocodile let Father Sparrow bathe in peace.

As for Father Sparrow, he and all his friends flew away and told their little wives all about the tug-of-war. Then they put their little heads under their wings and all went fast asleep. It had been a very busy day.

The Cat That Climbed the Christmas Tree

Chapter One : Elizabeth Ann's House

THERE was once a little girl whose name was Elizabeth Ann. Her home was an old grey house in an old grey town in the South of England. It was a big house with wide steps and pillars before the door.

Inside the door there was a square hall, with a great stove to keep it warm in winter time; and on three sides of the hall there were glass cases with stuffed birds in them. There were great hawks and owls, and even a black swan. Elizabeth Ann thought that very queer and interesting. Above them were stags' horns.

On the fourth side there was a wide stone staircase that led to the upper part of the house.

Upstairs there were long passages and a great many rooms, and at the other end of the house there was a wooden staircase called the back stairs. On wet days in holiday time the house was a lovely place to play *I spy*, and *Hide-and-seek*, and an exciting game called *Mother Bunch*. You could race up the front stairs and along the passages and down the back stairs, and nobody seemed to mind how much noise you made.

There were plenty of people to play, too. Elizabeth Ann had three sisters and two brothers, and there were always cousins as well. One Christmas Day there were seventeen boys and girls, and Elizabeth Ann's father and mother made nineteen people altogether. They stretched right across the road and pavements when they went to church that morning.

So you see they needed a very large Christmas Tree. It seemed a very tall tree to Elizabeth Ann, and it really was. Her father always had to climb high up the big stepladder to fasten the shining silver star to the top of the tree. While he was up there he fixed long chains of gold and silver paper, and set the little coloured candles on the upper branches.

While he was busy high up, the tall people helped a little lower down, and the short people helped a little lower still. Everyone used to be busy with the Christmas Tree, and when it was finished on Christmas Eve it looked most beautiful.

It stood right in the middle of the hall, and it sparkled and shone. There were bright threads of gold and silver, and bags of sweets, and flags and candles of all colours, and tiny looking-glasses and shining coloured balls among its branches.

Elizabeth Ann and all her cousins and sisters

"IT SEEMED A VERY TALL TREE TO ELIZABETH ANN."

Christmas Tree were left alone in the hall with the nice warm stove. It was very cold and frosty out-of-doors, and Mr. B. was glad to be warm and comfortable, but he was still puzzling about the Christmas Tree. Instead of lying by the stove, he walked round and round and looked at it.

Presently everyone came in from church and had dinner. Mr. B. had some too. He had a little chair to himself by Elizabeth Ann's father, but he had his real dinner afterwards.

When dinner was over everyone went to finish tying up the presents before hanging them on the Christmas Tree. Mr. B. was left all alone in the hall again. He felt that he really *must* find out about that queer tree.

What do you think he did?
He got up and stretched himself. He came over to the Christmas Tree. He got on to the big pot that held it, and he began to

climb. Perhaps he expected to find a mouse, or perhaps he thought that birds live at the top of a Christmas Tree.

Up and up he went. He had to go very slowly because the boughs were thick. On the way he pushed his fluffy grey head between the twigs, and sniffed at the queer smell of candles and flags and sweets.

The farther up he went, the less he liked it. He wanted to come down, but there seemed so many things in the way. He was afraid to jump for fear he should be tangled in the gold and silver chains of paper and all the shining gold and silver threads.

Chapter Three : Father to the Rescue

AT last Mr. B. felt he really could go no farther, and began to cry : " Meeow ! Meeow ! "

Everyone was busy tying up parcels, but Elizabeth Ann heard him.

" What is the matter with Mr. B. ? " she said.

Soon the others heard him too, and they all came out of their rooms and ran down the staircase together, all looking for Mr. B.

They could hear Mr. B. saying, " Meeow, Meeow," but no one could see him. The hall was dark, but there was a warm red glimmer from the stove, and they could see he was not lying there. They lit the gas and looked, but they could not see him anywhere in the hall.

At last they looked at the Christmas Tree, and there he was. He looked like a fluffy grey caterpillar, holding on very tightly and calling for help with all his might.

Elizabeth Ann's father got the tallest stepladder and set it by the Christmas Tree, and climbed up and took hold of Mr. B. Very gently he pulled away his little grey paws.

"Poor Mr. B.!" he said.

Mr. B. climbed on to Father's shoulder, and took hold of it with all his claws, and came riding down the step-ladder safe and sound. Then he jumped down and shook himself, and sat down by the stove and washed himself all over. He didn't like the smell of Christmas Tree!

Everyone else went back and finished wrapping up the presents, and put them on the tree, and under the tree, and round the tree; and then they all had tea and Christmas cake.

Afterwards they lit all the candles and danced round the Christmas Tree and sang, *Here we go round the Christmas Tree* instead of *Here we go round the Mulberry Bush*.

Mr. B. sat by the stove and watched them all. He never climbed a Christmas Tree again. He knew everything that he wanted to know about Christmas Trees.

QUESTIONS

The Tale of a Turnip (page 7)

1. Say what a turnip is like, and draw one. How is a turnip different from a carrot?
2. Where is the Mouse in the picture on page 11?
3. Pretend that they asked their friends to settle about the soup that was left. One friend spoke for each of them. Which would you speak for? What would you say?
4. Make this story into a little play to act. It is quite easy and great fun.

The Tale of the Harvest Bun (page 13)

1. Say what a harvest bun looks like and what is in it.
2. What made the mother drop the bun?
3. Each proper song in the story is longer than the one before. Why is that?
4. The last song is very short. Why?

The Little Brown Bird (page 25)

1. What trees come in the story? Which were the prettiest and the strongest? Which were the kindest?
2. Why was the little brown bird unhappy?
3. Where were his friends going? Why?
4. Pretend that you are the little brown bird in spring. Say something to each of the kind trees.

The Old Woman who Lived in a Vinegar-bottle (page 33)

1. Where was the Old Woman at the end of the story? Do you think she deserved it? Why?

2. Paint a picture of the first little house.

3. What did the Old Woman have to do to make her wish come true?

4. Which of her homes would you choose for yours? Why would you not choose the others?

Father Sparrow's Tug-of-War (page 45)

1. Why was Father Sparrow cross at first? What made him worse?

2. What kept the sparrows busy all the morning?

3. Which was the stronger, Elephant or Crocodile?

4. How did Brother Elephant keep steady when he was pulled extra hard?

5. Do you think they deserved to be treated so? Why?

6. Draw an elephant and a crocodile.

The Cat that Climbed the Christmas Tree (page 54)

1. How many brothers had Elizabeth Ann? How many sisters? How many children had her father all together?

2. What games did they play? Do you know all those? Tell how to play another game for wet days.

3. What was the cat called? Why? What colour was he?

4. Have you a cat? What colour is he? What is he called? Tell a story about him or another cat.

5. Draw a Christmas Tree in a pot on a stool. Make it look as pretty as you can.

2. Paint a picture of the first little house.

3. What did the Old Woman have to do to make her wish come true?

4. Which of her homes would you choose for yours? Why would you not choose the others?

Father Sparrow's Tug-of-War (page 45)

1. Why was Father Sparrow cross at first? What made him worse?

2. What kept the sparrows busy all the morning?

3. Which was the stronger, Elephant or Crocodile?

4. How did Brother Elephant keep steady when he was pulled extra hard?

5. Do you think they deserved to be treated so? Why?

6. Draw an elephant and a crocodile.

The Cat that Climbed the Christmas Tree (page 54)

1. How many brothers had Elizabeth Ann? How many sisters? How many children had her father all together?

2. What games did they play? Do you know all those? Tell how to play another game for wet days.

3. What was the cat called? Why? What colour was he?

4. Have you a cat? What colour is he? What is he called? Tell a story about him or another cat.

5. Draw a Christmas Tree in a pot on a stool. Make it look as pretty as you can.